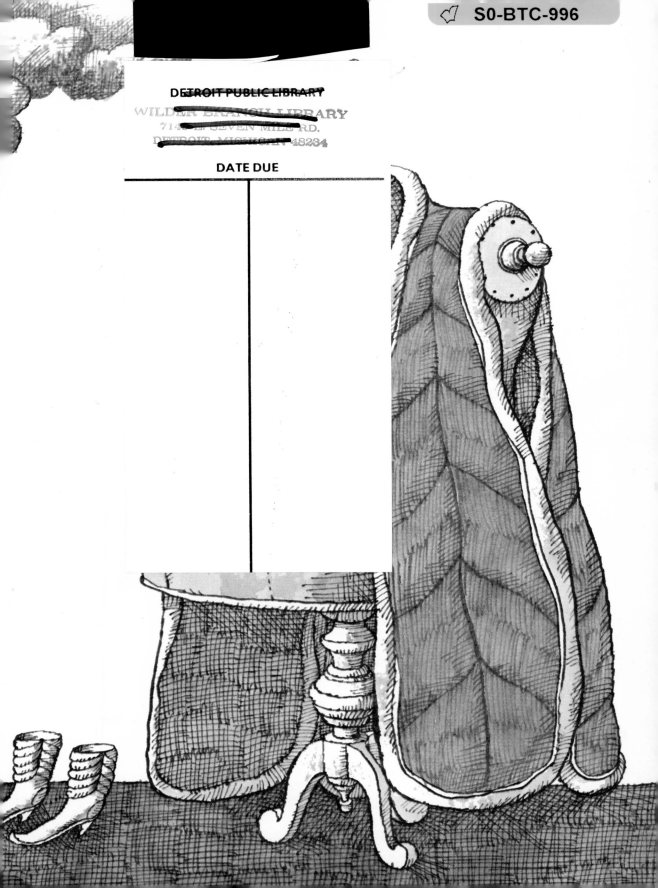

The Round Sultan
and the Straight Answer

by BARBARA K. WALKER
pictures by FRISO HENSTRA

PARENTS' MAGAZINE PRESS - NEW YORK

For Jeri and J. T. McCullen
who introduced me to the round sultan

Once there was and twice there wasn't a Turkish sultan who loved to eat. Three or five times a day he sat himself down at his dining table. One after another he ate yogurt soup and rice with yogurt and meats with yogurt and fruits with yogurt. Great heaps of dark brown bread simply melted away.

All around the sultan sat his courtiers, nibbling away at this and that. Musicians played. Beautiful veiled girls danced. A fountain splashed, and multicolored birds sang in their cages. Altogether, mealtimes were splendid times indeed.

Each day, the sultan was weighed in his royal set of scales. The sultan smiled to see that he was growing at last to be a fine figure of a ruler. He must surely be the fattest, roundest sultan in all the world, he thought.

But every good has its bad. One day the scales broke beneath his weight.

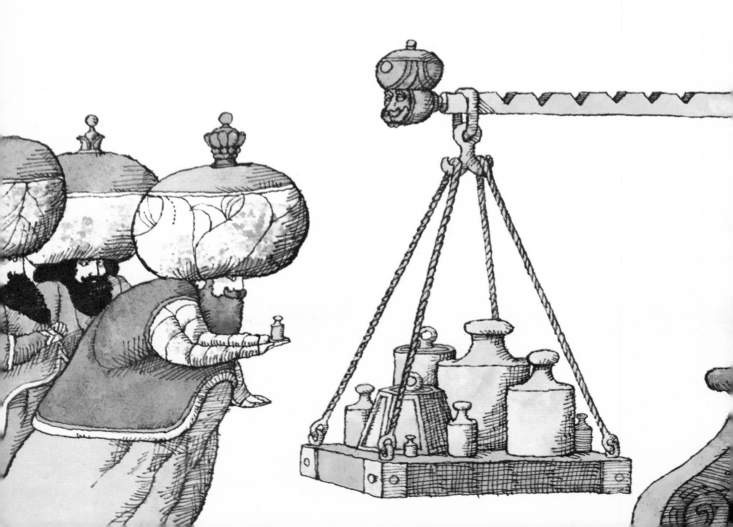

That day, too, the sultan discovered that he was too fat to walk a single step. His feet hurt hideously if he stood up even for a moment. His royal throne developed a crack which widened and widened. Finally the royal carpenters had to make another throne, twice as strong and sturdy as the first one.

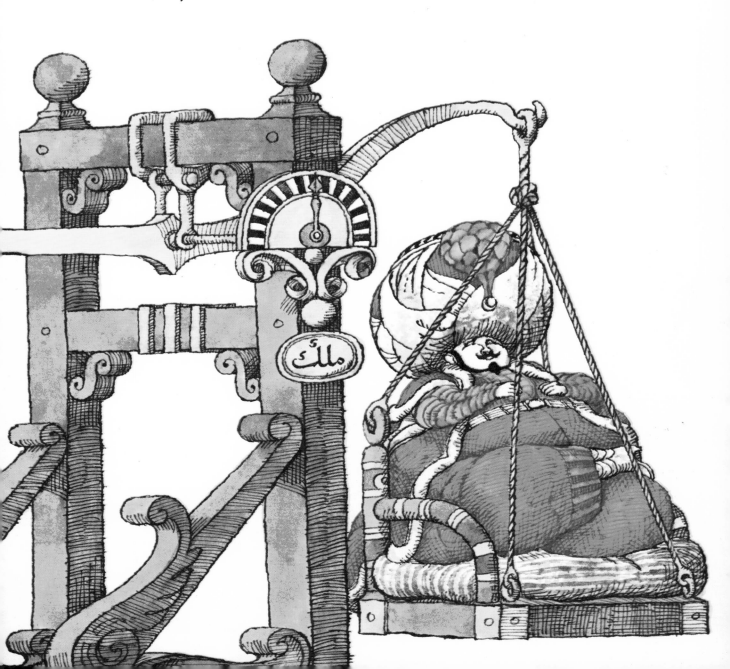

One by one, the sultan's royal shirts and royal trousers split at the seams. Tailors were called to make new clothes.

The sultan could no longer fit into the royal bathtub. A new one was made, large enough to bathe two full-grown buffaloes. Ten men helped the sultan into his bath. Ten men helped him out again.

Clearly, the sultan had become too fat. Something must be done before matters became any worse. Criers went out to the ends of the kingdom. "The sultan seeks a doctor. Who can help the sultan become thinner? Hear ye! Hear ye! Your reward will be great!"
Doctors hurried to the palace from all directions. Some brought books of healing. Some brought medicines. All of them were certain they could help the sultan.

The first doctor studied the sultan. Then he said solemnly, "My sultan, you must eat nothing but fruit." The sultan tried for seven days to eat nothing but fruit. He had fruit for breakfast, fruit for lunch, fruit for afternoon tea, and fruit for dinner. He *tried* to eat nothing but fruit. Oh, he ate between meals, now and then — a heap of rice with chicken made a pleasant snack. And nothing tasted better than a tray of honeyed baklava. At the end of a week, the first doctor came to examine the sultan. Alas, the sultan was fatter than ever. "To prison with him!" roared the sultan. "Give him nothing but fruit. As for me, fruit simply won't do."

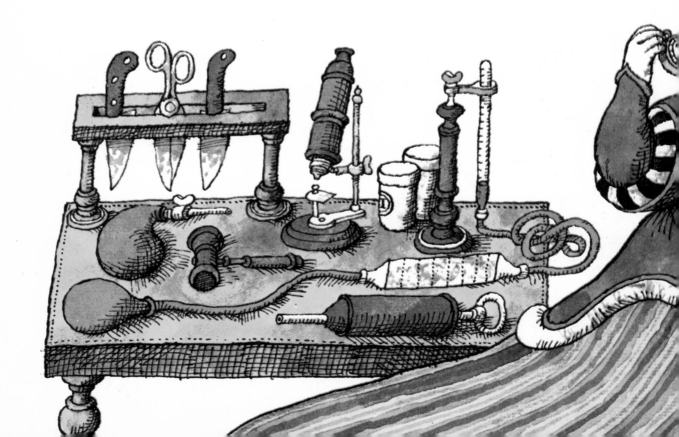

A second doctor studied the sultan. Then he said solemnly, "My sultan, you must take nothing but hot tea without sugar." The sultan tried for seven days to take nothing but hot tea without sugar. He had hot tea without sugar for breakfast, hot tea without sugar for lunch, hot tea without sugar for afternoon tea, and hot tea without sugar for dinner. Oh, he ate between meals now and then, because he was so hungry. A heap of rice with chicken made a tasty snack. And he *did* relish honeyed baklava. At the end of a week, the second doctor came to examine the sultan. Alas, the sultan was fatter than ever. "To prison with him!" roared the sultan. "Give him nothing but hot tea without sugar. As for me, hot tea without sugar simply won't do."

More doctors came. "Give the sultan steam baths every day," said one. The sultan steamed and steamed. Between steam baths he ate and ate. And off to prison went another doctor.

"Exercise!"

"Nothing but meat!"

"Smaller helpings!"

"No music and dancing at meals!"

"No company at meals!"

"Less sleep!"

"Nothing but yogurt!"

"Massage him and pummel him four times a day!"

"Give him these special pills!"

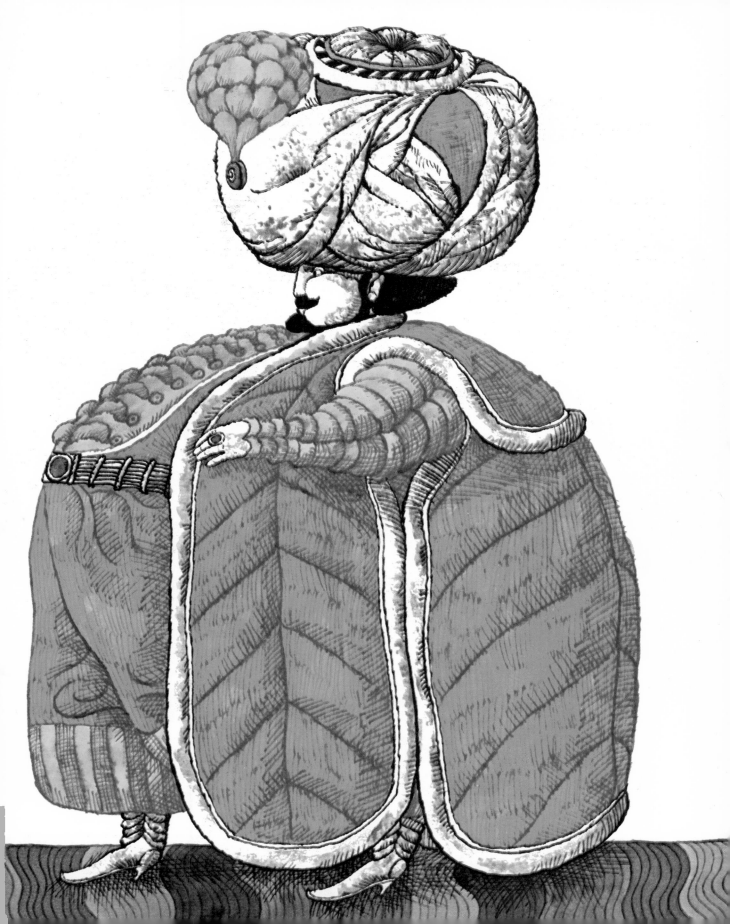

One after another, forty doctors tried their remedies. One after another, off to prison they went, each one condemned to his own remedy. As for the sultan, he grew fatter and fatter.

Then one day a clever hamal chanced to pass the palace. On his back he carried the furniture of a whole house. "Hamal!" called the sultan's vezir. "You are needed in the palace."

The hamal set down his burden. He hurried after the vezir. At last they arrived before the sultan. "You can carry the furniture from a whole house," said the vezir. "Lift our sultan into his bed."

For a moment the hamal studied the sultan. He had heard about the sultan's problem—*everybody* had heard about the sultan's problem. The hamal said boldly, "What does it matter whether he sits on his throne or lies in his bed? He will be dead in another forty days anyway!"

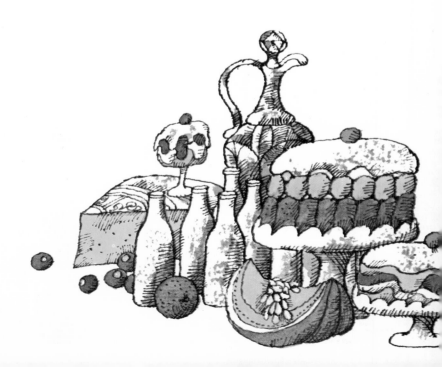

The sultan gasped. "How dare you!" he shouted. Then, in a voice scarcely louder than a whisper, he asked, "How do you know?"

"I just *know*," answered the hamal. "Believe me. You will be dead in forty days."

"He lies! Take him off to prison," ordered the sultan. And two servants dragged the hamal down the winding stone steps to the dungeon.

As for the sultan, suddenly he had lost his appetite. Only forty days more to live! He gnawed at his lips. He bit his fingernails. He groaned and sighed.

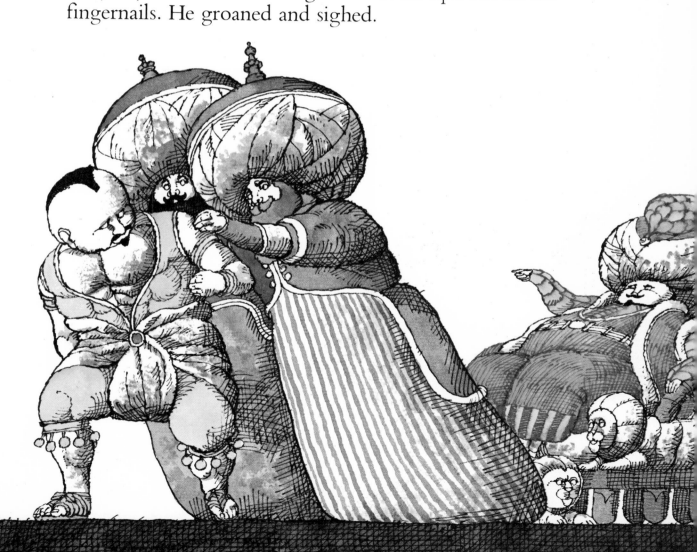

At breakfast he nibbled at toast.
At lunch he had a bit of white cheese.
At afternoon tea he sampled a plum cake.
At dinner he forced down a small kebab.
As for eating between meals, somehow food didn't seem important anymore.
Day after day passed. The sultan sat and worried. At the end of the twentieth day he arose. His feet felt numb, but he could walk again. He paced the floor hour after hour. Only twenty days more to live!
His royal shirts and his royal trousers sagged and bagged. Something strange had happened to them. They were *much* too big.

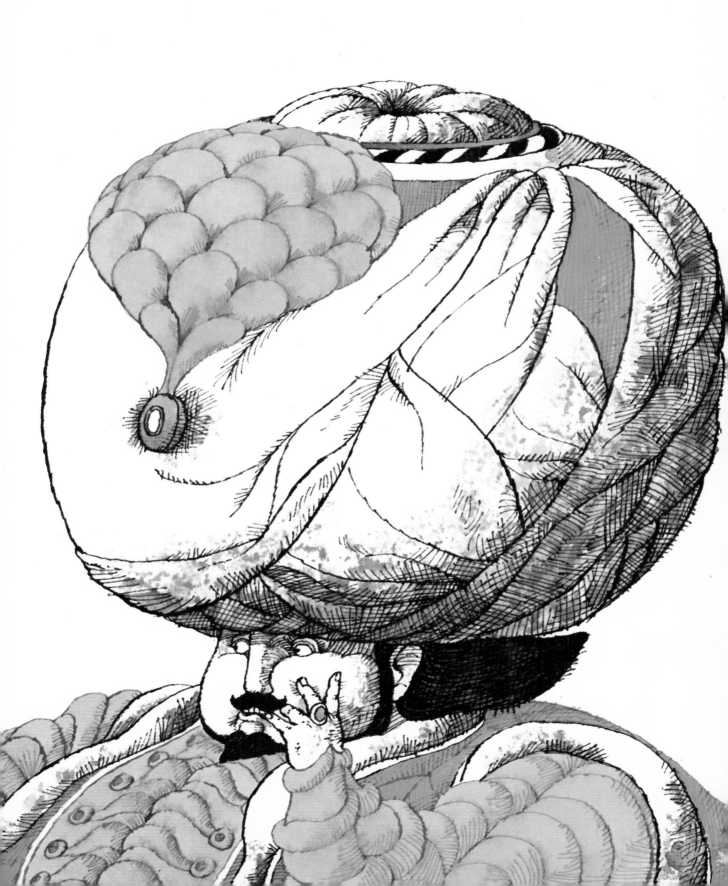

At the end of the thirty-ninth day, the sultan called his vezir. "Tomorrow I shall die," he said. "You must write out my last will and testament." He sighed as he passed the kingdom on to his younger brother. Who would have thought that the fattest sultan in the world would have ended in such a way?

The fortieth day came and went. All day the sultan

paced the floor, from the east windows to the west windows, from the north windows to the south windows. He sighed as he gazed out at the rows of houses below. What a pity to leave such a fine kingdom! But tonight was to be his last.

The forty-first day dawned sunny and bright. From the minaret came the familiar call to prayer. Birds sang in the trees of the sultan's garden. The sultan awoke.

He rubbed his eyes sleepily. Then suddenly he sat up. This was the forty-first day! He was still alive. "Praise be to Allah!" he rejoiced. "Send for that hamal!"

The vezir himself hurried down the stone steps to the dungeon. Forty doctors, all of them thin as thin, bowed as the vezir entered. The hamal arose. "Sire," he said, "this is the forty-first day."

"You are right," agreed the vezir. "The sultan has sent for you."

The hamal followed the vezir up the winding steps. What would happen now? What could he say to the sultan?

"There you are!" exclaimed the sultan, propping himself up in bed. "You said I was to die in forty days. This is the forty-first day. You lied!"

"That may be," answered the hamal. Then his eyes twinkled. "But see, sire, you are thin!"

For a moment the sultan was speechless. Then a great smile spread across his face. He leaped out of bed. He waltzed about the room in his flapping royal pajamas. He felt his thin arms, his thin legs, his thin neck. Yes, he *was* thin.

"Bring me a new pair of scales!" he shouted.

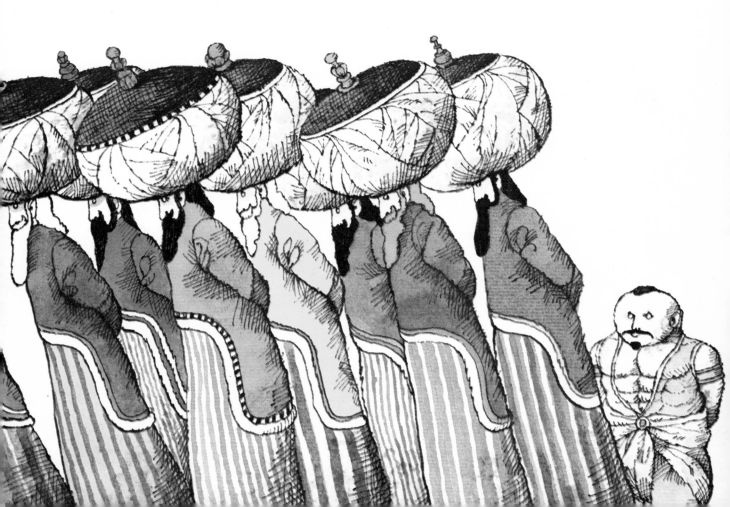

The servants hurried in with the stoutest pair of scales
in the kingdom. The sultan stepped into the dish at one
side of the scales. "Now fill up the other dish with gold
until the scales exactly balance," he ordered.
And the servants piled gold by the handful into the
dish until the great heap exactly balanced the smiling

sultan. "This gold, hamal, is your reward for your great wisdom," declared the sultan. "Take it, and may your way be open."

The hamal gathered up his treasure and with a thankful heart left the palace. One by one, the forty doctors climbed the stone steps and went about their business. As for the sultan, he became no fatter than a sensible sultan should be. And as far as I know, he is ruling yet.